the UnDeRDOgS

UNHAPPY CAMPERS

By Tracey West

ILLUSTRATED BY kyla may

SCHOLASTIC INC.

Copyright © 2022 by Scholastic Inc.

All rights reserved. Published by Scholastic Inc., *Publishers since 1920*. SCHOLASTIC and associated logos are trademarks and/or registered trademarks of Scholastic Inc.

The publisher does not have any control over and does not assume any responsibility for author or third-party websites or their content.

This book is a work of fiction. Names, characters, places, and incidents are either the product of the author's imagination or are used fictitiously, and any resemblance to actual persons, living or dead, business establishments, events, or locales is entirely coincidental.

ISBN 978-1-338-82736-1

10 9 8 7 6 5 4 3 2 1   22 23 24 25 26
Printed in Italy   183

First printing 2022
Book design by Jessica Meltzer

For Scott and John, two bold hearts and kind caretakers of dogs. —T. W.

I dedicate this book to my besties, Andy and Lara, whom I adore dearly. —K. M.

Table of Contents

Betty's Biscuits

OUR BISCUITS ARE EVEN BETTER THAN CARLY'S COOKIES!

NOVA

She's super **EXCITED** to meet you!

DOWNTOWN BARKSDALE
THE **BEST** DOWNTOWN, PAWS DOWN!

MANDY & RANDY
These twins are the **BEST** at being snooty!

OLLIE
He has the **BEST** cool tricks!

MS. FINELLA FINEFUR
She's the **BEST** principal!

CHEF WOLFGANG'S BISTRO

ARE WE THERE YET?

The fourth-year dogs from Barksdale Academy
were on their way to the yearly weekend trip
to Camp Ruffing It. The pups on the bus sang as
Coach Houndstooth drove them down the country
road. Everyone was happy and excited.

"If you're furry and you know it, wag your tail!

If you're furry and you know it, wag your tail!

If you're furry and you know it

1

And you really wanna show it
If you're furry and you know it, wag your tail!"

Harley wagged her fluffy tail along with the song. She was excited about the trip, too—especially because she was with her three best buddies. Harley, Nova, Peanut, and Duke had been friends since they first started at Barksdale Academy. Everyone called them the Underdogs. That's because everyone in Barksdale was the best at everything, and the Underdogs . . . not so much.

Nova, the most positive Underdog, sang louder than anyone on the bus.

Peanut was too worried about what waited for them at Camp Ruffing It to sing. "Camping is so dirty," Peanut mumbled. "So much messy mud. And itchy plants . . ."

Duke was too queasy to sing.

"Why do we have to sit all the way in the back?" he grumbled. "It's so b-b-b-bouncy!"

"Because we're Underdogs," Peanut replied. "We never get the good seats."

"Well, *I* love the back seat because it means we all get to sit together," Nova said. Then she burst into a shout.

"Second verse, sounds like the first!"

The rest of the pups on the bus joined her.

"If you're furry and you know it, scratch your ears! If you're furry and you know it, scratch your ears!

If you're furry and you know it
And you really wanna show it
If you're furry and you know it, scratch your ears!"

Harley liked the song, but she didn't like sitting in the back seat, either. She didn't have a good view of the scenery outside. So while everyone else was singing, Harley got up and scooted into the seat in front of her to see what she could see.

"STOP SIGN!"

Harley moved to another window.

"BIRD!" she announced.

Excited, Harley moved to the next window.

"TALL TREE!" she yelled.

Harley didn't mean to, but she had accidentally yelled right into the pointy ear of Principal Finella Finefur.

From her spot next to Nurse Barkwell, Principal Finefur peered at Harley through her glasses.

"Harley, please calm down," she scolded. "Take your seat and stay there. We don't want to distract Coach Houndstooth while he's driving."

"Yes, Principal Finefur," Harley said. She made her way to the back row just as the other pups finished their verse.

Nova raised her voice. **"Third verse, better than—"**

Peanut turned to look at her. "Nova, how can you be so cheerful about this trip? We're being taken into the dangerous, dirty wild against our will! There will be stinging bugs, and lumpy sleeping bags—"

"And green fields, and fresh air, and blue skies!" Nova finished, with a dreamy look in her eyes. "I love camping! And if we work together, we can make this the best camping trip ever!"

Duke groaned. "Are we there yet?"

While her friends talked, Harley looked across Nova and through the tiny back window to try to see more cool things. Thinking of Principal Finefur's warning, she yelled inside her head instead of yelling out loud.

BALE OF HAY! BIRD! ANOTHER BALE OF HAY! ANOTHER BIRD!

Harley glanced around the bus. Her side of the road was getting a little boring.

Hmm. There's an empty seat next to Athena! I'll just move over there and then stay put.

Harley scooted across the aisle.

"Hi, Athena," she said to her friend. "Okay if I sit here?"

"Sure, Harley," replied Athena.

Harley hopped over her and into the window seat. Her ears begin to wiggle. Her whiskers began to twitch.

YELLOW FLOWER! RED BARN! FIELD OF DAISIES!

And then Harley saw something on the road up ahead. Something moving so very slowly that it was in danger of being hit by the rolling wheels of the bus. She yelled out loud.

TURTLE! STOP!

CHAPTER 2

POP! GOES THE TIRE

Harley's sudden, loud scream made Coach Houndstooth jump in his seat. He lost his grip on the steering wheel, and the bus swerved off the road. He pumped on the brakes.

BUMP!

BOOM!

PFFFFFFFFT!

The front right bus tire ran over a sharp rock as the bus lurched to a stop. The rock sliced a hole in the tire.

Coach Houndstooth stood up, shaking.

"Is everyone okay?" he asked.

"Is anybody hurt?" Nurse Barkwell asked.

Luckily, everyone looked fine, just shaken up.

"Whew! Sorry about that," Coach said. "I got startled."

"You do not need to apologize, Coach," Principal Finefur said. She turned to Harley. "I asked you to stay in your seat, Harley. And what on earth were you howling about so loudly?"

Harley felt everyone on the bus looking at her.

"I . . . I saw a turtle," she explained. "And the bus was about to hit it."

Coach Houndstooth peered out the window. "Well, whaddya know? There *is* a turtle out there!"

The pups all moved to the front of the bus to see the turtle. It was still crawling very slowly across the road.

"I suppose I'm glad I didn't r-r-r-run it over!" Coach Houndstooth said. "But, Harley, maybe you could take down the volume next time?"

Harley nodded. "Yes, Coach."

"Everyone get back to your seats!" Principal Finefur called out. "Coach Houndstooth and I need to check on the tires. It sounds like we have a flat."

Harley scurried back to her seat next to the Underdogs.

Maybe being in the back row isn't so bad after all, she thought. *At least nobody can stare at me back here.*

Duke still had his paws over his eyes. "Is it over yet?" he asked.

"It's fine, Duke," Nova assured him. "We'll be back on the road soon."

Duke moved his paws to his stomach. "That doesn't make me feel any better."

Harley slunk down in her seat.

"Oh, Nova, I know everyone blames me for the flat tire," she whispered to her friend. "And they're right. It's all my fault!"

"It's okay, Harley," Nova assured her. "You were just trying to help that turtle."

"I know, but it's so embarrassing," Harley sulked. "You know how it is. Everyone in Barksdale is so perfect, except for us! And I just know I'm going to be teased by—"

"Mandy and Randy are heading this way!" Duke warned in a loud whisper. "Duck!"

Harley slunk down in her seat, but she couldn't hide from the two floppy-eared twins. They glared at Harley.

"Nice going, Harley," Mandy said.

"Yeah, nice going," Randy echoed.

"Now we'll never get to Camp Ruffing It," Mandy added.

"Never!" Randy agreed.

"We'll be stranded out here in the middle of nowhere," Mandy said.

Harley stared at the floor. *I feel bad enough already,* she thought. *Why do these two have to make it worse?*

Then Nova spoke up.

"We're not going to be stranded, Mandy," Nova said. "I'm sure Principal Finefur and Coach Houndstooth know how to change a flat tire."

"I sure hope so," Mandy said. "Because if not, our camping trip is ruined, and it's all Harley's fault."

Randy nodded. "Yeah, Harley's fault!"

Peanut chimed in. "Hey, Mandy! What's that on your tail?" he asked, pointing.

Mandy craned her head to look at her tail.

"Ha! Made you look!" Peanut cried, and Mandy scowled at him.

"You didn't make *me* look," Randy said smugly.

"You're right," Peanut said. "Hey, Randy, are those crumbs in your fur?"

Randy turned to look at his back. "Ew! Where?"

Peanut grinned. "Made *you* look this time!"

"Hmpf!" Mandy huffed.

"Hmpf!" Randy grunted.

The twins turned tail and went back to their seats. Harley sat up straighter.

"Thanks, Nova. Thanks, Peanut," she said. "I didn't feel like standing up to those mean doggos."

Duke looked at her. "I'm not good at standing up to them either, Harley."

"That's why you have me and Nova!" Peanut said. "We won't let anyone mess with our friends."

"That's right! We Underdogs have to stick together," Nova added. "Paws in!"

The four friends put their right paws together. "UNDERDOGS FOREVER!" they cheered.

Coach Houndstooth and Principal Finefur came back onto the bus.

"We r-r-r-replaced the flat tire with the spare," Coach announced. "It's smaller than the other tires, though, so we may be in for a bumpy ride."

"We're not far from Camp Ruffing It. I know you're all excited, but I expect everyone to be on your best behavior for the rest of the ride," Principal Finefur warned.

Coach Houndstooth started the engine. "Hold on to your tails, tots!"

THUMP!

The bus rolled back onto the road.

BUMP!

The bus wobbled forward on the wonky wheel.
Duke grabbed his stomach again.

"Ugh!" he wailed. "This is even worse than before!"

Harley felt another pang of guilt. *Mandy and Randy were right. This is my fault*, she thought. *I've got to figure out how to control myself on this camping trip!*

Then a bird flew by her window, and her
nose twitched . . .

You can do it, Harley, she told herself. *Or, like Nova
would say, you can at least try your best!*

CHAPTER 3

PUP TENT PROBLEMS

BUMP. BUMP. BUMP!

The bus limped down the road and finally pulled into the parking lot of Camp Ruffing It. Coach Houndstooth turned off the engine.

We made it! Harley thought. *I didn't ruin everyone's camping trip after all!*

Principal Finefur stood up.

"Now, students, we will disembark in an orderly—"

23

"GET ME OFF THIS BUS!" Duke howled, and he bounded down the aisle and out the door. Then he got on his knees and kissed the ground.

"We're here, we're here, we're finally here!" he cheered.

The rest of the pups got off the bus in an orderly manner, just as Principal Finefur instructed. They lined up in front of the baggage compartment to get the backpacks holding their gear for the weekend: sleeping bags, extra clothes, snacks, and other items.

Coach Houndstooth tossed out the backpacks one by one. Harley's tail began to wag with excitement. This trip was going to be fun!

"Mandy! Randy! Ace! Ollie! Athena! Duke! Pea—oof!"

Peanut had packed a huge piece of luggage on wheels. It was almost twice the size of Coach Houndstooth! The coach struggled under its weight as he pulled it out of the compartment.

"Peanut, what in the name of all that is furry do you have in here?" he asked.

Peanut padded forward.

"Just the essentials, Coach," he replied. "Fur shampoo, fur spray, tail detangler, snout scrubber, canine comfort mattress . . ."

"Good gravy, young pup, you know you're supposed to be r-r-r-ruffing it, right?" Coach Houndstooth asked.

"I *am* roughing it! My gaming chair wouldn't fit, and neither would my mini fridge!" Peanut protested. "Ruffing it isn't for everyone, you know."

Coach shook his head. "Carry on, Peanut."

The little dog hopped on top of his suitcase.

"Duke, a little push please?" Peanut asked.

"No problem, dude!" Duke replied, and he easily pushed the heavy luggage across the grass.

"Harley!" Coach called out. Harley caught the backpack tossed to her. Then she gazed around the camp.

The heart of the camp was a green meadow with one large wooden building. The sign out front read KIBBLE CABIN. Near that was a firepit with tree stumps and logs to sit on all around it. A dense forest surrounded the meadow, and Harley saw signs for hiking trails and a lake.

But that wasn't all Harley saw. Her sharp eyes saw a chipmunk darting under a bush. Her sharp ears heard the flapping of a butterfly's wings. Her sharp nose smelled trash-scented raccoon breath coming from the Kibble Cabin.

So . . . many . . . critters! she thought. She was about to explore the raccoon smell when Principal Finefur's voice rang through the fresh air.

"All right, students! Three of you are assigned to each pup tent, and I've divided you into groups. First, Nova, Harley, and Athena. Come get your tent!"

Nova picked up the pup tent and began to bound toward the meadow.

"Wait for us, Nova!" Athena cried. She and Harley raced to catch up. "First we need to determine the best location for our tent. A spot with sun in the morning and shade in the afternoon. Away from poisonous plants. On top of a slope in case it rains."

Harley and Nova looked at each other and smiled. Their friend Athena was always thinking!

"Sure, Athena!" Nova said.

Athena nodded. "Excellent. Now let me see . . ."

Athena trotted off, and Nova and Harley followed her, carrying the tent. Athena moved from one spot to another, wiggling her nose each time she stopped.

"Athena, why do you keep wiggling your nose like that?" Harley asked.

"It helps me think," Athena replied. Then she grinned. "This is a good spot. Let's put up the tent!"

Nova emptied the bag holding the tent, and a bunch of poles slid out.

Harley frowned. "How are we supposed to make a tent out of this?"

"I'm sure we can figure it out together!" Nova replied.

Athena grinned. "Or, we could read the instructions that were in the bag," she teased.

The three friends got busy, sliding the poles together and pushing them into the ground. Then it came time to stretch the fabric over the poles.

"Harley, hold this pole right here while Nova and I pull the fabric over it," Athena instructed.

"Sure!" Harley said, and she grabbed the pole.

Nova and Athena fiddled with the fabric.

"I think it's supposed to go this way!" Athena said.

"Maybe it's that way!" Nova said.

Harley gazed across the meadow again while her friends worked on the tent. Most of the other pups had their tents up already, but some were still working. Nearby, she spotted Duke and Ollie putting the finishing touches on their tent. Next to them, Peanut was jumping up and down.

Boing! Boing! Boing!

Harley watched him, fascinated. *What is Peanut doing?* she wondered.

Then something next to Peanut began to inflate: a big, puffy couch! Peanut stopped jumping.

"Whew! All done!" he said, and he hopped onto the couch and leaned back.

Coach Houndstooth walked by, stopped, and shook his head. "Peanut, this is definitely not r-r-r-ruffing it!"

"Ruffing it isn't for everyone," Peanut repeated, and the coach walked away.

Curious, Harley bounded over to him. "Peanut, what is that? Did you seriously bring a couch on a camping trip?"

Then Harley heard something behind her.

CRASH!

Harley whirled around. The tent had collapsed on Nova and Athena!

"Oh no!" Harley cried. "I was supposed to be holding the pole!"

CHAPTER 4

TAKE A HIKE!

Harley bolted back to Nova and Athena. Nova climbed out from under the collapsed pup tent.

"Oh, Nova, I'm so sorry!" Harley cried. "Peanut was jumping up and down, and I wanted to see what he was up to, and—"

"It's okay, Harley," Nova said. "I know you didn't mean for the tent to fall on us."

"Hmpf hmpf hmpf hmpf mmm hmmmm!"

Harley's ears twitched. "Did you hear something?"

"Can somebody please help me?" Athena asked, poking her head out from under the tent fabric. "I'm all tangled up!"

Harley and Nova helped untangle Athena. The fluffy little dog jumped back on her feet.

"Let's try this again," she said. "But this time, *I'll* hold the tent pole."

The three of them got back to work and soon had their pup tent set up. As they stashed their gear inside, they heard Coach Houndstooth's whistle.

TWEET!

"All r-r-r-right, pups! Before lunch, let's go on a quick hike to work up our appetites! Line up at the start of the tr-r-r-rail!"

"Hooray, a hike!" Nova cheered.

"That sounds like fun," Harley said.

The campers all made their way to the trail. Everyone looked happy and excited. Ace Swiftrunner, the fastest student in year four, led the pack. Mandy and Randy jogged behind him, wearing matching bandannas.

Peanut and Duke trotted up to Harley, Nova, and Athena. Ollie, who had wheels strapped to his back legs, rolled up with them.

"Ugh. What's fun about a hike?" Peanut asked. "It's just a lot of stomping around in dirt and getting all sweaty!"

Duke, who didn't mind dirt but was afraid of almost everything else, frowned. "I hope we don't see any snakes. Or spiders. Or lizards."

Ollie whirled around on his wheels. "I just hope the trail isn't too bumpy. Bumps can be tough on my wheels."

"Well, I hope our hike isn't dirty, scary, *or* bumpy," Nova said. "I hope it's just right."

Harley's whiskers started to twitch. "Maybe we'll see lots of cute critters on this hike. Like furry little bunnies. And more chipmunks with chubby cheeks . . ."

"R-r-r-ready, pups?" Coach Houndstooth asked.

"Ready!" everyone replied.

"Gr-r-r-reat!" cheered Coach Houndstooth. "Now, Principal Finefur and Nurse Barkwell are staying at camp. So all eyes on me. Keep your nose clean, your tail close—and whatever you do, don't stray off the path!"

Coach Houndstooth led the pups into the woods.

"All right marchers, r-r-r-repeat after me," he began. "I don't know but I've been told."

"I DON'T KNOW BUT I'VE BEEN TOLD!"

"Barksdale pups are brave and bold."

"BARKSDALE PUPS ARE BRAVE AND BOLD!"

"Bark off!"

"WOOF! WOOF!"

"Bark off!"

"WOOF! WOOF!"

"Bark off, one, two, three, four . . ."

"WOOF WOOF!"

They marched through the woods. Harley peered through the leaves. She sniffed the air. She perked her ears. But she didn't see, smell, or hear any critters.

All that shouting must have scared them away, she figured.

She fell into step with the other dogs and watched her friends.

Athena was examining a flower with her magnifying glass.

Ollie was rolling along smoothly.

Nova's tail wagged happily as she marched.

Duke slowly plodded along, keeping an eye out for snakes.

Peanut clung to Duke's neck, trying to climb onto his back.

"What kind of trail is this?" Peanut complained. "It's full of itchy branches and scratchy brambles."

"What's a bramble?" Nova asked.

"I'm not exactly sure, but I think it's that sharp thorny thing that keeps poking me in the butt!" Peanut answered.

Duke sighed. "Do you seriously want me to carry you for the whole hike?"

"You can do it! Nobody's stronger than you!" Peanut said. "Besides, I'll keep an eye out for snakes from up here."

Duke nodded. "Fine, Peanut." Then he grunted and moved to catch up to the front of the line.

Athena walked over to Harley. "There are so many fascinating plants here!" she said. "I've counted three different species of wild herbs already."

"Hmm, that's nice," Harley said. Plants were okay, especially if you could eat them, but definitely not as exciting as critters. Cute critters, fuzzy critters, skinny critters, leggy critters, hopping critters . . .

I love to chase them, she thought, *and play with them, and sometimes nibble on their fluffy tails . . .*

Then her ears perked up. She heard something.

SQUEAK!

She turned her head toward a nearby tree. There, sitting on one of the roots, was a chipmunk! A cute little, furry little chipmunk.

Is that the same chipmunk I saw when we got to camp?
Harley wondered.

"Hey there, little chippy!" Harley called out, and
she jumped off the path toward the chipmunk.

SQUEAK!

The chipmunk darted away and Harley followed it, running in circles around a patch of weedy
brambles.

"I just want to play!" Harley cried.

TWEET!

Coach Houndstooth blew his whistle. "Harley, get on the path right now!"

"Yes, Coach!" Harley cried, and she bounded back to join her friends.

Randy and Mandy marched past her.

"Coach said stay on the path, Harley. Don't you ever listen?" Mandy asked.

"Yeah, don't you listen?" Randy echoed.

Harley frowned as they marched away.

"What did you see out there, Harley?" Nova asked.

"A chipmunk," Harley replied, scratching behind her right ear. "A cute little, furry little chipmunk."

"I don't blame you," Nova said. "Chipmunks *are* very cute."

Harley scratched behind her left ear. "Yes, they are," she replied. Then she scratched her back.

"Are you okay, Harley?" Duke asked.

"Sure. Why?" Harley asked, scratching the top of her head.

"Hmm," Athena said. She trotted over to the edge of the weedy path. Then she frowned.

"I've got bad news for you, Harley," she said. "You and that chipmunk were just playing in a patch of poison ivy!"

CHAPTER 5

SCRITCH SCRATCH!

"**P**oison ivy?" Harley asked.

"Poison ivy?!" Coach Barksdale barked. "Harley, don't you touch anyone. Pups, let's turn ar-r-r-round and get back to camp. Looks like we've got to cut our hike short."

"Hooray!" Peanut cried as he clung to Duke's back.

"Whew!" Duke said, looking relieved.

Nova shook her head at Peanut as they hiked back to camp. "Peanut, this is nothing to cheer about. Poor Harley's got poison ivy!"

"It's not so bad," Harley said, scratching behind her ear. Then she scratched under her chin. Then her back felt itchy, but her short legs couldn't reach the itchy part. She frowned. "Okay, maybe it is bad. I'm really, really itchy!"

"I'm sure Nurse Barkwell has something in her first-aid kit that can help," Nova reassured her.

Athena, meanwhile, was slowly walking along the edge of the path. Then she started to pluck small orange flowers growing on long stems.

"First-aid kits are great, but nature has a remedy for poison ivy," she said. "This jewelweed should do the trick."

Harley scratched the back of her neck. "I'll try anything!"

"We're almost back at camp. Let's ask Nurse Barkwell first," Nova suggested.

They soon emerged from the woods.

TWEET!

"Everyone to the Kibble Cabin for lunch!" Coach Houndstooth called out. "Everyone, that is, except for Harley, who will report to the first-aid tent."

Harley sighed.

Athena gave the orange flowers to Harley. "Bring these to Nurse Barkwell. She'll know what to do."

"Thanks," Harley said, and she nodded to Nova, Duke, and Peanut. "I'll catch up with you!"

Peanut pointed toward the Kibble Cabin. "Onward, Duke!"

"Um, dude, you can get down now, you know," Duke said.

"Do I have to?" Peanut asked. "This is really convenient."

WHOMP!

Duke quickly plopped down on the grass, and Peanut tumbled off his back.

"Okay, I get the hint," Peanut said, brushing grass off his fur. "See you later, Harley!"

Harley laughed, almost forgetting how itchy she was. But she scritched and scratched the whole way to the first-aid tent.

"That's definitely poison ivy, Harley," said Nurse Barkwell after she examined her. "How did that happen?"

"I was playing with a chipmunk," Harley replied.

Nurse Barkwell smiled. "Chipmunks are so cute and furry, aren't they? I've seen jewelweed growing in these woods, and luckily—"

"Athena picked some," Harley said, handing over the bunch of flowers.

"Excellent!" Nurse Barkwell said. "Give me a minute to prepare these."

Harley scratched and scratched some more as Nurse Barkwell pounded the plant into a gooey green paste in a large bowl. Then she handed it to Harley.

"First you need to wash off," she instructed. "There's an outdoor shower behind the Kibble Cabin. Then apply the paste—and leave it on!"

"Thanks!" Harley replied, and she dashed to the Kibble Cabin, holding the bowl in one paw and scratching her fur with the others.

The sound of laughter floated out from the cabin, and a yummy smell hit her nose. Her stomach grumbled.

"Mmm, smells like burgers!" she said. "I hope they save one for me!"

She turned on the water and soaped up her fur. The itching calmed down a little as she scrubbed.

When she finished, she turned off the water and shook out her fur. Then she peered into the bowl of green glop.

"Here goes nothing," she said, and she dipped her paw in the goop. She sniffed. It smelled . . . fresh. Not too bad. She patted it behind her ears and smiled.

"Ahhh," she said. "That's kind of soothing."

Harley patted the paste from the tips of her ears to the tip of her tail. It was already starting to dry into a crackly green mess.

Harley's stomach grumbled again.

"Burger time!" she said, and she bounded to the Kibble Cabin.

But when she opened the door, the cabin was empty. Everyone else had eaten lunch and left. And even worse, there were no burgers left on the food table!

"Ugh!" Harley moaned. "If I hadn't chased after that chipmunk, I'd have a belly full of burgers right now. When will I ever learn?"

CHAPTER 6

THE LAKE MONSTER

Nurse Barkwell stepped into the Kibble Cabin.

"There you are, Harley," she said. "How are you feeling?"

"Less itchy," Harley replied. "But more hungry! I missed lunch."

"Oh, that won't do," Nurse Barkwell said. "Let me see what I can find you in the kitchen."

The nurse returned a few minutes later with a paper bag and handed it to Harley.

"I found some kibble bars and carrot sticks," she said. "You can munch on those when you catch up to everyone. They're down at the lake. I'll walk you there."

"Yay! Swimming!" Harley said happily.

Nurse Barkwell shook her head. "Not for you. You have to leave that paste on for an hour, Harley. But you can enjoy the fresh air while you wait."

"Gee, that sounds like fun," Harley mumbled. "But I guess I have nothing better to do."

Harley grabbed a towel from her pup tent, and she and Nurse Barkwell took the path to the lake.

A sandy shore surrounded the lake. Its deep blue, murky water glimmered in the afternoon sun. Campers swam, splashed, and played while Coach Houndstooth watched.

TWEET!

"No swimming past the yellow markers, pups, or you'll be benched faster than a hound can gobble up a peanut butter biscuit!" Coach yelled.

Harley put down her towel.

"Remember, Harley, one hour!" Nurse Barkwell said, and then she took the path back to camp.

Harley sat on her towel and sighed. She ate one kibble bar. It tasted like sawdust. Then she ate a carrot stick. It tasted like, well, carrots, which was better than sawdust but not as tasty as burgers.

She gazed out at the water. Nova and Ace were jumping off the dock in the middle of the lake. Duke was pushing Peanut and Ollie around on an inflatable raft. Everyone looked like they were having a great time.

Buzzzzzz!

Her ears twitched at the sound of a sky raisin flying past her on its tiny wings. Her head snapped to the right and she gulped it down.

Better than a kibble bar, she thought. She listened for another sky raisin but didn't hear one.

Harley lay back on her towel and waited for the hour to be up. She waited. And waited some more. Then she dozed off.

"IT'S A LAKE MONSTER!"

Harley woke up to the sound of Duke and Peanut shouting. They were pointing at her.

"It's the legendary Creature of Camp Ruffing It!" Duke cried.

"The creature from the bottom of the lake!" Peanut added. "So green and slimy!"

Harley laughed. "Dudes, it's me, Harley! Nurse Barkwell gave me this green paste for my poison ivy."

Duke and Peanut squinted.

"It sounds like you, Harley," Duke said.

Peanut took a step closer and gave Harley a long look. "It *is* her!" he replied. "Bummer. I thought we were snout-to-snout with a real live monster!"

Harley stood up and started slowly and stiffly marching toward the boys.

"I am the Lake Monster-r-r-r," she growled.

"Very funny, Harley," Peanut said.

Harley stretched her front paws out in front of her. "I AM THE LAKE MONSTER, AND I AM HUNGRY!"

Peanut stuck his tongue out at her. "Ha! Too bad you can't catch me!"

Harley chased Peanut down to the lake. They ran through the shallow end, splashing up water with their paws.

Suddenly, Harley froze. She remembered Nurse Barkwell had said to stay out of the water for an hour. *I'd better get back to my towel*, Harley thought.

Then Harley saw a sparkle of silver swimming through the water from the corner of her eye.

Fish!

CHAPTER 7

ONE . . . TWO . . . THREE!

Harley ran after the fish. As soon as she reached the deeper water, she ducked under and swam. The glimpse of silver was always just out of reach. She swam and swam until she ran out of breath. Then she came up from under the water, gulping for air. The green paste began to fall off her fur.

TWEET! TWEET! TWEET!

"Harley, you are out of bounds! Get back here this instant!" Coach Houndstooth called out.

Harley blinked and looked around. She had swum past the floating yellow markers bobbing on top of the water.

"But, Coach, I didn't mean—"

"Right now, Harley!"

Harley slowly and sadly swam back to shore. The green glop continued to fall off her fur as she swam.

"Ew! Harley's slimy!" Mandy cried.

"Really slimy. Gross!" added Randy.

Harley frowned as she walked back onto shore.

"On your towel until we go back to camp, Harley," Coach Houndstooth told her.

Harley sighed. "Yes, Coach."

Harley shook the last of the green paste and water from her fur and went back to her towel. Nova bounded up to her.

"Hey, Harley," she said. "What happened out there?"

"I saw a fish in the water. When I swam after it, I went past the markers without realizing it," Harley explained.

"I get really excited about things, too, sometimes," she said. "Want me to hang out with you while you're benched?"

"That's okay. You shouldn't have to stop having fun just because I messed up," Harley replied.

Nova gazed out at the lake. Harley could tell she really wanted to go back there.

"Go, Nova!" Harley leaned back on her towel. Then she told a little fib so her friend wouldn't feel bad. "I'm kinda tired anyway. I'll just take a little nap."

"Well, if you're sure . . ." Nova said.

Harley closed her eyes and pretended to sleep.

ZZZZZZZZ! ZZZZZZZZ!

"Ha! Ha! See you later, then!" Nova called, and ran back to the water.

As soon as Nova was gone, Harley opened her eyes and sat up. She wasn't sleepy at all. She didn't feel very itchy anymore, and she really wanted to be out there in the lake with her friends.

"Why do I always have to do everything wrong?" she asked with a sigh.

"You don't do everything wrong, Harley. You do most things right!"

Harley turned to see Nurse Barkwell behind her.

"I came back to check on you, and I overheard you," the nurse said. "Don't be so hard on yourself, Harley. Everyone makes mistakes."

"Nobody in Barksdale makes mistakes except for the Underdogs," Harley pointed out. "And I make a lot of them. It happens every time I see any kind of critter. All I can think about is chasing after it."

Nurse Barkwell nodded. "I know! Whenever I see something cute, or fuzzy, or furry, or leggy, or hoppy, I want to chase it, too."

Harley's eyes widened. "Really?"

"Sure," Nurse Barkwell replied. "And that used to get me into a lot of trouble. It still does, sometimes."

"So what did you do?" Harley asked.

"Well, when I see a cute critter, I close my eyes, take a deep breath, and count to three," the nurse replied. "That usually works."

"Because it calms you down?" Harley asked.

Nurse Barkwell grinned. "Yes. But also because the critter is usually gone by then," she replied. "And Harley, there are a lot of critters here at camp. And a lot of dangers that you won't find in Barksdale. So try to be more careful the next time you see a critter, okay?"

Harley nodded. "Okay. Thanks, Nurse Barkwell."
TWEET!
"Out of the water, pups!" Coach Houndstooth barked. "Back to camp for some fr-r-r-ree time and a cookout!"

Nova, Duke, and Peanut ran up to Harley.

"You're not a monster anymore!" Peanut said.

"How are you feeling, Harley?" Duke asked.

"Hungry! I missed lunch, and now I can't wait for that cookout!" she answered.

They made their way back to camp. Along the way, Harley saw a flash of yellow in a tree.

Bird! she thought, and her tail wagged in anticipation of the chase. Then she remembered what Nurse Barkwell had told her, and she closed her eyes.

"One, two . . ."

"Harley, what are you doing? Sleepwalking?" Peanut asked.

Harley's eyes snapped open. "Oh, nothing," she said quickly, and she glanced back at the tree. The yellow bird had flown away, and she let out a sigh of relief.

The camping trip got off to a ruff start, she told herself. *But you can turn things around, Harley. You can do better!*

When they got back to camp, they saw Principal Finefur building a campfire in the large firepit. The table next to her was piled with long sticks and platters of sausages.

"Mmmm," Harley said, her mouth watering. "I hope we have the cookout soon!"

"Not too soon," Peanut said. "I need some time to relax with my paw massager."

"Paw massager?" Nova asked.

They followed him to the boys' pup tent, where Peanut dragged out a round device that looked like a little pool. He pressed a button and a fountain of water shot up from the middle.

"Battery powered," he said. Then he dipped his front paws in the pool. "Ah, that feels good after a long day of hiking around."

"Dude, I'm the one who was hiking *you* around," Duke said. "Let me try!"

Duke put his front paws in the massager. "Mmm, that *does* feel good!"

Nova and Harley shook their heads and headed for their tent.

"I'm going to get the book of constellations I brought with me," Nova said. "We should be able to see a lot of stars tonight."

"Sure," Harley said. "I'll wait for you by the fire. I don't want to be late for the cookout!"

As Nova trotted away, Harley spotted something in the grass.

The chipmunk!

The tiny creature spotted Harley and stood up on its hind legs. Harley was about to move toward it, but she stopped and closed her eyes instead.

One . . . two . . . three!

She opened her eyes, and the chipmunk was still there. Except now it was doing a handstand! Harley took a deep breath and closed her eyes.

One . . . two . . . three!

Harley opened her eyes, and now the chipmunk had its back to her, and was waving its tail back and forth.

It wants to play! Harley bit her lip and closed her eyes.

One . . . two . . . three!

This time, the chipmunk was running in circles around her. Harley could not resist. She leapt toward the chipmunk.

"I'll play with you!" she cried.

The chipmunk raced past the firepit, moving like a streak of lightning. Harley picked up speed, trying to catch up.

BAM!

Harley banged into the table next to Principal Finefur—and the platters of sausages tumbled into the dirt!

CHAPTER 8

THE CREATURE IN THE WOODS

"**H**arley! Stop running this instant!" Principal Finefur cried.

Harley froze, and her furry cheeks got warm. Everyone was staring at her. Tears sprang into her eyes.

"Dinner is ruined!" a pup wailed.

Mandy pointed at Harley. "Don't you mean that *Harley* ruined dinner?"

"Yeah, Harley ruined it!" Randy added.

"I—I didn't mean it!" Harley stammered. "I'm sorry!"

Principal Finefur took a deep breath. "Harley, running around a fire is a bad idea," she said. "We're lucky that only the sausages got hurt! I was saving some special kibble bars for us to eat our last night at camp. We can eat them for dinner tonight instead."

All the campers groaned.

Coach Houndstooth interrupted.

"Keep your tails up, camper-r-r-rs!" he said. "First, let's all work together to clean up this mess. When the sun goes down, we'll tell scary stories around the campfire!"

Everyone grumbled and began to pick up the scattered sausages. Harley helped, and then she slinked off to her pup tent. Nova and Athena spotted her and followed.

"Harley, come back to the campfire!" Nova said. "What you did was an accident. Everyone understands."

"Not Mandy and Randy," Harley pointed out.

"True. But still, you shouldn't let them spoil your night," Athena said. "The stars tonight are going to be bright in the clear sky. The Dog Star will be right above us!"

Harley sniffled. "That does sound nice," she said. Then she shook her head. "It's no use. I might as well stay in the tent for the rest of the trip. I keep ruining things for everyone!"

"You've got a point," Athena said, and Nova nudged her.

"You're being too hard on yourself, Harley," Nova said.

Harley shook her head. "No, it's true. I can't control myself at camp. There are too many cute critters here! Way more than in Barksdale. Nurse Barkwell tried to help me, but I just can't stop myself when a critter makes my nose wiggle, or my ears twitch, or my eyes blink."

Nova looked thoughtful. "Harley, your love of critters is a big part of who you are," she said. "But it's true that camp is a lot different than Barksdale. Maybe you can just try to chase after critters a little more carefully."

"Carefully?" Harley asked.

"You know, like maybe not so fast, and try to be aware of things around you so you don't bump into them," Nova said. "I know what it's like to knock things over, you know. It might not be easy, but you can try."

Athena nodded. "Maybe a key word would help. Like, when your brain screams, 'Critter!' you can think, 'Careful!'"

"Hmm," Harley said. "We tried that when we practiced for our K-1 exam back in Barksdale. It didn't work then, but I'm really trying to do my best on this trip. So I'll try again!"

Nova grinned. "Great! Now let's get back to that campfire!"

When they joined the rest of their friends, the sun was setting and the first stars were starting to appear in the dark blue sky. All the pups were talking and laughing and munching on kibble bars and apples.

Harley felt relieved. Everyone seemed to have forgotten about the spilled sausages already.

They settled in around the campfire next to Duke, Peanut, and Ollie. Peanut was chilling out on an inflatable armchair.

"You look comfy, Peanut," Nova remarked.

"Yeah, this camping thing isn't so bad, if you know what to bring," Peanut said, looking up at the sky.

Mandy and Randy walked up to the Underdogs and their friends with their noses in their air.

"Well, look who it is," Mandy said.

"Yeah, look who it is," said Randy.

"It's the Underdogs!" Mandy cried. "Scaredy Duke. Clumsy Nova."

"Persnickety Peanut. And Harley who ruins everything!" Randy finished.

Peanut jumped off his chair. "Who are you calling per-per—"

"Per-snick-et-y," Athena said slowly. "Randy is saying you are very fussy about things."

Peanut frowned. "That may be true, but I'm still insulted," he said. "Why don't you just scram, Mean Mandy and Rotten Randy?"

"We're not going anywhere," Mandy replied. "It's almost time for scary campfire stories."

Mandy and Randy pushed in front of them and took the spots closest to the fire.

"How s-s-s-scary do you think the stories are going to be?" Duke asked, nervously clutching his stuffed duck, Mr. Quacky.

"I don't like scary stories either, Duke," Athena said. "I'm just going to look up and try to spot the Dog Star!"

"I think I'll watch the stars with you two," Harley said. *If I'm watching the stars, maybe I won't notice any critters!* she thought.

"Attention, pups, it's time for some fun!" Coach Houndstooth barked. His paws were filled with long, skinny sticks and a giant bag of marshmallows. "It's mar-r-r-rshmallow toasting and scar-r-r-ry story time! Gr-r-r-rab some sticks and settle in!"

The pups grabbed their marshmallow-toasting sticks and passed the bag of marshmallows around. Then they all held the marshmallows over the fire until they became nice and golden.

"Who wants to tell a scar-r-r-ry story?" Coach Houndstooth asked.

Mandy and Randy's paws shot up. "We do! We do!"

Coach Houndstooth nodded, and the twins leaned closer to the fire. The flames made spooky shadows on their faces.

"This is the story of the watcher in the woods," Mandy began.

"The watcher in the woods," Randy repeated.

"Many years ago, the first campers came to Camp Ruffing It," Mandy said. "And one very dark night, they went for a hike in the woods."

"They didn't know it, but something was watching them. A creature with glowing yellow eyes crept out of the woods and followed them," Randy continued.

Duke nudged Athena and Harley. "Can we look at the stars now?"

Athena nodded. "Just look up, Duke. We don't have to listen."

"And the glowing yellow eyes got closer . . . and closer . . ." Mandy continued.

Harley looked up at the stars, too. They twinkled in the night sky.

Then, out of the corner of her eye, she saw two eyes glowing in the nearby bushes. She gasped. They looked just like the eyes in the spooky story!

". . . then the creature of the woods revealed itself," Randy said. The other pups leaned forward. "It was a . . ."

Harley's ears twitched. She heard a faint chitter-chatter from the bushes. It sounded like a—

"CHIPMUNK!" she screamed. Her little friend had come back out to play.

Then she remembered what Athena had told her, and thought: *Careful!* But it was too late.

Harley's scream had already frightened the campers.

Mandy and Randy tumbled backward into several sticky marshmallows.

Duke jumped into Peanut's inflatable chair.

BOING!

Peanut went flying into the air.

Nova chased after him. "I'll catch you!"

While all this was happening, Harley *carefully* ran toward the bushes, dodging a furious Randy and Mandy and sidestepping Nova, who caught Peanut with both paws.

"I'm coming, my chipmunk friend!" she called out.

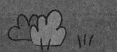

EW!

"I'm here, little buddy!" Harley cried as she pushed aside the bushy leaves.

Chitter-chatter!

A critter stuck its head out the bush. But it wasn't a chipmunk. This critter had a white stripe running down the middle of its black furry face and a tuft of white fur on top of its head.

"A skunk!" Harley cried happily. "Come here, you little cutie!"

The skunk squeaked loudly, then turned and showed Harley its black-and-white tail.

"What a pretty tail you have!" she said.

The skunk lifted its tail and . . . sprayed Harley!

"Wait, don't go!" Harley cried as the skunk scurried away. Then she sniffed.

I stink of skunk! she realized.

The smell had never bothered Harley that much. In fact, she kind of liked it. But she knew that most pups thought it was a terrible smell.

"I am *not* going to ruin everyone's night with this skunky smell!" she promised. "I'll just sneak back to my pup tent."

Harley headed toward the tent, staying in the shadows as she walked past the campfire.

"THERE SHE IS!" Mandy cried.

"THIS IS ALL HER FAULT!" Randy added.

Harley froze as someone shone a flashlight on her. She could see Peanut staring sadly at his deflated chair. Mandy and Randy had marshmallow stuck to their fur.

"Harley, please come here," Principal Finefur said.

"Um, I really need to go back to my tent," Harley said.

"Not yet. We need to discuss what just happened," Principal Finefur insisted.

Harley felt everyone's eyes on her as she stepped toward the campfire. Mandy stomped up to her.

"Harley, why did you—EW!" Mandy cried, grabbing her nose.

Everyone seemed to get a whiff of Harley at the same time.

"EWWWWWWWWWWWWWWWWW!"

Principal Finefur stepped back. "Stay where you are, please, Harley. Nurse Barkwell will attend to you. Everyone else, please report to the Kibble Cabin."

Nova hung back. "I wish I could stay with you, Harley. But I've got a very sensitive snout when it comes to skunk. It makes my eyes water and my nose gets a stinky overload!"

"I tried to be careful, like Athena said," Harley said. "I saw the glowing eyes and I heard the chitter-chatter, and I thought it was my chipmunk friend. I approached it very carefully, but it turns out it was really a skunk instead."

Nova sighed. "It's okay, Harley. I'll see you later, okay?"

Nova ran off to join the other pups as they filed into the Kibble Cabin.

"MOVIE TIME!" Coach Houndstooth shouted from inside, and the pups let out a cheer.

Harley sighed again. "No movie for me, I guess."

Just then, Nurse Barkwell appeared, holding a big plastic jug. It had a picture of a skunk on it. The skunk was inside a red circle with a line through it.

"This Skunk-a-Way will help get rid of the stink, Harley," Nurse Barkwell said. "But first—"

"Back to the shower," Harley said with a sigh.

She took the jug from Nurse Barkwell and went back to the outdoor shower behind the Kibble Cabin. As she lathered up, she could hear the others inside enjoying the movie. Harley recognized it as one of her favorites: *The Furriest Bride.*

"We'll never find those peanut butter biscuits!" cried the brave Princess Butterpup.

"Nonsense!" said the dashing hero, Woofley. "You're only saying that because no one ever has."

Harley wished she could be inside with her friends! She rinsed off the Skunk-a-Way and then sniffed her fur. She could still make out the faintly stinky smell of skunk, but mostly she smelled fake flowers. Yuck!

Harley felt like crying. She was damp. She smelled icky. And she was all alone.

"Face it, Harley," she said out loud. "Your best is the *worst*!"

OPERATION BUDDYGUARD

That skunk made me too stinky to watch the movie with everyone. But at least I can go look at the stars, Harley thought.

She walked to a little green hill and sat on top. She looked up, hoping to see the Dog Star, but now clouds covered the sky.

"I guess I won't get to have any fun at all," she said.

"Of course you will! The fun squad is here!"

Harley turned to see Nova, Duke, and Peanut coming up the hill. Nova had a swimmer's nose clip on her snout. Duke had a clothespin on his nose. And Peanut wore a snorkeling mask!

"Don't you pups want to watch the movie?" Harley asked.

Duke shrugged. "That's okay. I've already seen it a million times."

"And you shouldn't be all alone, Harley," Nova said. "We Underdogs need to stick together!"

"Thanks," Harley said. "But maybe you shouldn't come near me. I'm a disaster! You pups can't even come close without wearing special gear."

"It's okay," Peanut said. "I think I look pretty cool in this. Like a super villain."

He made his voice sound deeper. "Princess Butterpup, I have kidnapped the peanut butter biscuit baker! The kingdom shall be biscuit-less!"

Nova pretended to be Princess Butterpup. "You won't get away with this, you horrible hound!"

Harley laughed. "I'm glad you're here. I *was* feeling lonely. But it's my own fault. I can't seem to stay out of trouble on this trip!"

"What exactly is the problem, Harley?" Duke asked.

Her friends listened as she explained how there were so many cute critters at Camp Ruffing It—and also so many new dangers, like campfires and itchy plants. Even though she'd tried staying focused, counting to three, and being careful, nothing had worked.

"Hmm," Duke said. "Maybe what you need is a bodyguard."

"A bodyguard?" Harley asked.

"Sure," Duke said. "We can take turns sticking close to you, and if you see a critter and start to run after it, we'll stop you."

Nova grinned. "That sounds more like a *buddy*guard!"

"That's an awesome idea! I'll have the best buddy-guards ever," Harley said. "Thanks, pups."

"Paws together, Underdogs!" Nova called out, and the four dogs piled their paws on top of one another. "Tomorrow, let Operation Buddyguard begin!"

Harley woke up the next morning feeling hopeful. She only smelled a *little* bit like skunk mixed with fake flowers.

Nova jumped up, her tail wagging. "Good morning, Harley! Your buddyguard is reporting for duty!"

Athena sat up and yawned. "Buddyguard?"

"Duke, Peanut, and I are going to be Harley's buddyguards today," Nova explained. "We're going to take turns sticking close to her, and when she sees a critter, we'll stop her from chasing after it."

"Hmm," Athena said thoughtfully. "I like the play on words. However, I'm not sure if this sounds like a good plan . . ."

"Where's your paw-sitive attitude, Athena?" Nova asked. "Come on, let's go to breakfast! It's time to put Operation Buddyguard in action!"

The three dogs stepped out of the pup tent into the morning sunshine. The other campers were making their way to the Kibble Cabin.

"Okay, Harley, we've just got to make it from here to the cabin without chasing after anything," Nova said. "I know you can do it."

Harley nodded. "Here we go!"

They walked to the cabin. Harley's ears began twitching to the sound of birds waking up in the woods. She took a deep breath and counted silently in her head.

One . . . two . . . three.

It worked! She didn't run off into the woods.

And I didn't even need my buddyguard, she thought proudly.

She was about to tell Nova the news when her ears twitched again. This time she heard a rustling sound near the Kibble Cabin. A *chitter-chatter*. She sniffed the air. She knew that smell—a smell that excited her even more than the sweet smell of a fluffy chipmunk.

"RACCOON!" she cried. Harley loved raccoons' cute little masked faces, and their furry tails, and their little paws that loved to search through garbage. She hardly ever got to see raccoons in Barksdale.

Harley took off running toward the dumpster, and Nova took after her. Nova ran fast, but Harley was faster. She reached the dumpster first and jumped—

BAM!

Nova caught up to Harley and tackled her before she could dive in. The two dogs tumbled onto the grass.

WHOOSH!

The frightened raccoon jumped out of the dumpster and fled into the woods.

Nova stood up, panting.

"Sorry, Harley," she said. "I tried to stop you before you took off, but you're too fast."

"That's okay, Nova. You tried!" Harley said. She gazed off sadly into the woods. "Where did you go, little raccoon?"

Athena trotted up to them. "This is what I predicted," she said. "Harley exceeds her friends in speed and agility. I don't think any of you will be able to stop her once she starts chasing something."

"I'm not ready to give up on Operation Buddyguard yet," Nova said. "Let's turn things over to Duke."

Inside the Kibble Cabin they found Duke, Peanut, and Ollie eating kibble cereal and bananas. The girls piled food into their bowls and joined them at their table. They found Peanut brewing a drink in a fancy little machine.

Coach Houndstooth walked past, stopped, and shook his head. "Almond milk lattes in the Kibble Cabin? Do you call that ruffing it, Peanut?"

Peanut took a sip from his steaming cup. "Ruffing it isn't for everyone," he replied, and the coach kept walking.

"Why is your fur so messed up?" Peanut asked Nova and Harley.

"Operation Buddyguard: Phase One failed,"

Nova explained. "Duke, it's your turn to be Harley's buddyguard. I wasn't fast enough to stop her, but you're strong enough."

Duke slurped down the last of his cereal and stood right behind Harley. "If you want to chase any more critters, Harley, you've got to get past me."

Harley nodded. "Thanks, Duke!" she said. "I need all the help I can get. Today is the last day of camp, and I don't want to mess it up!"

CHAPTER 11

PEANUT'S PLAN

Harley tried to relax a little bit while she ate breakfast. It helped to know that Duke was going to be her buddyguard. She dug into her kibble cereal and talked with her friends.

"I'm pretty hyped up for the canoe trip today," Ollie was saying.

"Yeah, it sounds like fun—as long as I don't get splashed on," Peanut replied.

Harley wanted to concentrate on the conversation, but she couldn't.

Don't think about critters. Don't think about critters, she told herself.

Chitter-chatter!

Harley froze. The sound was coming from behind her. She slowly turned her head to see a chipmunk perched on the open windowsill.

"CHIPMUNK!"

Duke quickly moved behind Harley, blocking her path. Harley knew she couldn't knock Duke over, so she sprang up on her back legs and leapt clear over him!

"Oh no," Duke said.

Harley raced toward the back of the Kibble Cabin. Duke, hadn't stopped her, but . . .

TWEET!

"Harley, stop this instant!" Coach Houndstooth barked.

She stopped in her tracks. Coach Houndstooth approached her.

"There is no running in the Kibble Hall," he said sternly. "If I catch you out of line again, you won't be coming on the canoe trip."

Harley nodded. "Yes, Coach."

Harley walked back to the table with her head down. Duke looked at her sadly.

"Sorry I failed you, Harley," Duke said.

"That's okay," she replied. "You tried."

"This once again proves my hypothesis was correct," Athena piped up. "Harley can outrun any of us. It is impossible to stop her once she sees a critter."

"Maybe phase one and phase two failed, but now it's my turn!" Peanut announced.

Athena looked at him. "No offense, Peanut, but if Nova and Duke couldn't stop Harley, how can you?"

Peanut grinned. "I have a plan."

TWEET!

"All r-r-r-right, pups! Time to go to the river for our canoe tr-r-r-rip!" Coach Houndstooth announced.

The pups filed out of the Kibble Cabin. Peanut walked closely beside Harley.

Nova gave them a pup talk. "We just need to get Harley to the river without her running off first," she said. "I know you can do it, Harley!"

"I've got this," Harley said, trying to sound confident. But the truth was, she didn't *feel* confident. It seemed like all she could think about now was critters!

Coach Houndstooth started a chant as they walked.

"The pups go marching one by one!"

"HURRAH! HURRAH!" the pups responded.

"They howl and bark at the moon and sun!"

"HURRAH! HURRAH!"

Harley chanted along, smiling. For a few minutes, she didn't think about critters. Then, under the sound of the chant, she heard something else.

RIBBIT! RIBBIT!

Her ears twitched. "Frog!" she cried.

"**BUNNY!**" Peanut yelled.

Harley stopped. "Wait, what?"

"**HEDGEHOG!**" yelled Peanut.

"Wait, where?" Harley asked.

Peanut pointed to the right. "There."

"I don't see anything," Harley replied. "But I hear a frog, over—"

Peanut pointed to the left.
"MOOSE!"
Harley spun around. "Moose? Are you kidding?"
She was starting to feel confused. And a little dizzy. As they marched on, Peanut kept pointing left, then right. Then left, then right.

"FOX!"

"SQUIRREL!"

"WOODPECKER!"

"GORILLA!"

Harley stopped. "Gorilla? What are you trying to do, Peanut, confuse me?"

Peanut grinned. "Exactly. And I can't think of any more woodland critters, so it's a good thing we're here."

Harley stopped and looked around. They'd reached the river! A row of green canoes was lined up on the river bank.

"Good job, Peanut and Harley!" Nova cheered. "Phase Three of Operation Buddyguard was a success!"

"Um, I guess," Harley said. "I mean, we got here, but I feel weird and dizzy. I can't have Peanut around me all the time, confusing me."

"It's just for the rest of the trip," Nova said. "One more night."

TWEET!

"All r-r-r-right, pups!" Coach Houndstooth called. "It's three of you to each canoe! Stick to your pup tent groups."

Harley frowned. "That means I won't be in a canoe with Peanut!"

"It's okay," Nova said. "I'll still be your buddy-guard. I won't try to confuse you, like Peanut did, but I'm sure everything will be fine."

Harley gazed down the river, at the rushing water teeming with fish and frogs, and the overhanging tree branches filled with chirping birds. The sound of unseen creatures going chitter-chatter and pitter-patter filled her ears.

This is going to be a disaster! she thought.

CHAPTER 12

A HOWLING WE WILL GO

Everyone put on their life jackets. Coach Houndstooth and Principal Finefur got into a canoe and gave a quick lesson on how to paddle.

"Those in the front and the back of the canoe will control the oars," Principal Finefur began. "First, grab the oar firmly in your paws . . ."

Harley sat in the middle of the canoe between Nova and Athena. The rhythm of the rowing practice soothed her a little bit. But still, she was very worried.

What if I ruin this canoe trip for everyone?

Nova saw the worried look on her friend's face and stopped rowing.

"Harley, everything's going to be okay," she said. "It's a beautiful day. No matter what happens, you are Harley and you are awesome exactly the way you are."

Harley let out a deep breath. Her friend's words made her feel a little better.

TWEET!

"All r-r-r-right, campers! Let's bring these canoes into the water!" Coach Houndstooth called out.

The pups obeyed and soon the canoes were floating smoothly along the river. Harley relaxed and looked up at the puffy white clouds floating in the bright blue sky. She took a deep breath. The sounds of the bubbly breath of fish, the croaking of frogs, and the chitter-chatter of forest critters faded into the back of her mind.

Principal Finefur led the campers in a song.

"A HOWLING we will go, a HOWLING we will go, HIGH HO the DOGGY-O, a HOWLING we will go!"

Harley sang along with the others as they launched into the second verse.

"A growling we will go, a growling we will go, high ho the doggy-o, a growling we will go!"

As they rowed and sang, Harley noticed many critters. Two otters frolicked in the water. A turtle sunbathed on a rock. Two chirping chickadees flew overhead.

Harley kept singing. She didn't chase after any of them.

Until . . . she spotted something up ahead. Something different.

Suddenly, Harley jumped out of the canoe and into the water! Her canoe tumbled over, spilling Nova and Athena into the river.

Coach Houndstooth blew his whistle. "Har-r-r-rley, **STOP!**"

CHAPTER 13

LAND HO!

Harley didn't stop. She swam past Coach Houndstooth and Principal Finefur's canoe.

"Harley, swimming in the river is dangerous!" Principal Finefur called out.

Harley kept swimming. She swam to the riverbank, to what she had spotted from her canoe: a beaver.

The beaver was gnawing on the trunk of a tree that was bending over the water.

"Stop, beaver!" Harley cried, climbing up the bank. "That tree is about to fall!"

The beaver stopped, saw Harley, and then turned and fled. Harley scooted under the tree and propped it up with her back.

"I'll hold it up while everyone passes!" she called out.

Coach Houndstooth and Principal Finefur looked up at Harley, surprised.

"Quickly, everyone!" Principal Finefur called to the campers. "Harley can't hold up the tree forever."

The canoes rowed past Harley and the tree. In the last canoe were Nova and Athena, their fur dripping wet.

Harley waited until they rowed past. Then she jumped into the water and climbed back into her canoe. The tree fell into the water behind them with a huge splash.

"Harley, you saved us all from that tree!" Nova cheered.

"Yes, that was quick thinking," Athena agreed.

"Thanks," Harley said. "When I saw that beaver chewing on it, I knew the tree might fall and hit one of our canoes."

Duke, Peanut, and Ollie rowed up next to them.

"Way to go, Harley!" Peanut said.

"Trees falling is one of my fears," Duke admitted. "So is riding in boats. And beavers. But with you around, I'm a lot less afraid. Thanks, Harley."

Harley smiled. "Thanks, dudes!"

TWEET!

"Uh-oh," Harley said. "Do you think I'm in trouble?"

But Coach Houndstooth wasn't blowing his whistle at Harley.

"Land ho! Island up ahead! Time for a break!" he cried.

The river opened up in front of them, and a small island sat in the middle of it. The pups beached their canoes and climbed up onto the shore. Principal Finefur opened up a cooler of pup-sicles and handed them out.

Duke took his and flopped down on the ground. "It feels good to be on solid ground again!"

"Agreed, dude," Peanut said. "My fur is ruined from all that splashing!"

Nova laughed. "Athena and I got a serious dunk when Harley toppled the canoe."

Just then, Coach Houndstooth and Principal Finefur approached.

"We need to speak to you, Harley," Principal Finefur said.

Harley gulped.

"We just want to thank you for your quick thinking back there," Coach Houndstooth began.

"I'm not in trouble?" she asked, her eyes widening in surprise.

"Harley, we know this trip has been challenging for you," Principal Finefur replied. "But today I think we all learned that the way you notice things around you—and your love of critters—can be very helpful sometimes."

"That tr-r-r-ree would have knocked me right on my noggin!" Coach Houndstooth grinned. "Thank you, Harley."

Harley smiled. "You're welcome!"

"Just maybe try to stay away from skunks,"
Principal Finefur advised.

Ace bounded up with Mandy and Randy behind him.

"Harley, that was awesome!" Ace said. "I didn't even notice that beaver."

"Yeah, thanks, I guess, Harley," Mandy said reluctantly.

"Thanks," Randy echoed.

Harley felt a warm, fuzzy, furry feeling. "I guess I'm just good at noticing things."

The pups enjoyed their break and soon got back on the water in their canoes. Nova started a chant, and the Underdogs and their friends joined in.

"I don't know, but I've been told!"

"I DON'T KNOW, BUT I'VE BEEN TOLD!"

"My friend Harley's brave and bold!"

"MY FRIEND HARLEY'S BRAVE AND BOLD!"

Peanut chimed in.

"Harley chases after critters!"

"HARLEY CHASES AFTER CRITTERS!"

"Tried to stop, but she's no quitter!"

"TRIED TO STOP, BUT SHE'S NO QUITTER!"

Duke finished up.

"Bark off!"

"WOOF! WOOF!"

"Bark off!"

"WOOF! WOOF!"

"Bark off, one, two, three, four . . ."

"WOOF WOOF!"

Harley beamed with pride as her friends sang.

"I just tried real hard and did my best," she told them. Then she grinned as she thought of a rhyme. "I finally passed this camping test!"

THE DOG STAR

The sun was setting as the dogs made their way back to camp at the end of their canoe trip. Harley's stomach growled loudly.

"Bear!" Duke cried.

"No, just my empty stomach," Harley said with a laugh. "I hope we'll be able to eat something tonight besides kibble bars."

Mandy and Randy trotted up to the Underdogs.

"If there's no cookout tonight, it'll be all your fault anyway, Harley," Mandy said.

"Yeah, your fault," Randy echoed. "She knocked over all the sausages yesterday. Who knows what's left to eat?"

"I'm really sorry about that," Harley said. "I know everyone's really hungry, and—"

Nova stopped and sniffed the air. "Wait!" she cried. "I'd know that smell anywhere!"

All the dogs started sniffing.

"CHEF WOLFGANG'S PIZZA!" everyone yelled, and they stampeded toward camp.

Chef Wolfgang's mobile pizza truck was set up by the campfire, and pizzas were bubbling on top of a slab in a wood-fired oven.

"Chef Wolfgang, what are you doing here?" Coach Houndstooth asked.

"Yesterday I got a call from one of my best customers: Peanut," Chef Wolfgang replied. "He told me about your sausage mishap and the story pulled at my heartstrings. So I am providing pizzas for all you campers tonight!"

The pups cheered.

Coach Houndstooth looked at Peanut. "Pizza around the campfire, Peanut?" he asked. "I call *that* awesome!" Then he started helping Chef Wolfgang hand out plates.

Peanut grinned. "I guess ruffing it isn't for everyone!"

Harley hugged Peanut. "Thank you! Now everyone will forget that I spilled the sausages."

Peanut shrugged. "Nova's right. We Underdogs have to stick together," he said. "Besides, I am so sick of kibble bars!"

The tired but happy campers settled around the campfire with their pizza. They sang songs and told spooky stories. Harley was so happy that she didn't think about critters even once. She thought about how lucky she was to have such good friends who'd tried to help her stay focused. And who loved her even when she failed.

When the last story was finished, the pups all looked up at the sky and watched the stars.

"Look, it's the Dog Star!" Athena cried, pointing at the sky. "That big, bright star is the nose of the constellation Doggus Majorus."

The dogs got quiet as they traced the path of the stars, starting from the Dog Star.

"Granny Goldenfur says if you make a wish on the Dog Star, it will come true," Nova said.

"Let's all make a wish," Duke suggested.

Harley closed her eyes and tried to think of a wish.

Chitter-chatter!

Her ears twitched as she heard the sound of a critter nearby. But she didn't run. Instead, she opened her eyes and looked up at the Dog Star.

"I have the perfect wish," Harley said. "That the Underdogs will always stick together!"

ABOUT THE AUTHOR

TRACEY WEST has written more than 300 books for kids, including the *New York Times*–bestselling Dragon Masters series for Scholastic Branches. The canine companions Tracey has known during her life have all served as inspiration for the Underdogs. She currently lives in New York State with her husband and adopted dogs.

KYLA MAY is an Australian illustrator, writer, and designer. She is the creator and illustrator of the Diary of a Pug and Lotus Lane book series and illustrator of *The Sloth Life: Dream On*. Kyla has also contributed her imagination and talent to six animated TV series, as well as toys and gifts for children of all ages. Kyla lives by the beach in Victoria, Australia, with her three daughters, three dogs, and two cats.